The Secret Mermaid

Turtle Trouble

Sue Mongredien

Illustrated by Maria Pearson

First published in the UK in 2010 by Usborne Publishing Ltd., Usborne House,
83-85 Saffron Hill, London EC1N 8RT, England. www.usborne.com

A CIP catalogue record for this book is available from the British Library.

FMAMJJASOND/19

ISBN 9781409506355 02961-3

Printed in India

Contents

Molly

Shanti

Eloise

Leila

Undersea Kingdom

Queen Luna

Aisha

Iona

Phoebe

Chapter One

"Dad! Gran! Guess what I've just seen!" Molly Holmes burst into the cottage, her cheeks pink from the cold December day. She kicked off her boots and dumped her coat on the side before running into the living room.

"Goodness!" her gran exclaimed, smiling. "Something exciting, obviously. What have you just seen?"

Her dad looked up from where he was sitting on the floor, building a tower of bricks with Molly's baby brother Toby. "Father Christmas?" he guessed.

"Nearly as good," Molly replied. "We were at the farm shop and Mum was chatting to someone for ages, so Annie, the farmer there, took me to see the baby chicks. And one hatched, right while we were watching! It was so cute."

She smiled, remembering how exciting it had been, watching as one of the eggs in the incubator had jiggled from side to side, and then how a small hole had appeared in the shell. She'd been able to see some movement from inside the egg…and then another crack had suddenly appeared and the hole became a bit wider.

Annie had explained that the chick was

tapping away from the inside with its beak to
make a bigger and bigger hole in the shell –
and just as she had said that, the eggshell had
cracked right open and there had sat a
bedraggled tiny chick, its feathers all damp
and its legs very wobbly as it tried to stand.

"Was it definitely a baby chick?" Dad joked. "Not a baby ostrich or baby...dinosaur?"

As soon as he said the word "dinosaur", Toby looked up. "Rrraaarrr!" he said excitedly, bashing the wooden bricks together. Toby was nearly one and had just started making a few animal noises. It was so sweet! Molly had taught him to say "woof-woof", "baa" and "moo", but his favourite noise of all was "rrraarrr"!

Everyone laughed. "Not 'rarrr', Toby, chicks go 'cheep cheep'!" Molly said.

"Rrraaarrr," Toby said stubbornly, and Molly laughed again and went to help her mum unpack the shopping in the kitchen. *Baby dinosaurs hatching from eggs, indeed,* she thought. Now that would be *really* exciting!

The smile slipped from her face, though, as she noticed the headline on the newspaper her mum had bought. *FEARS FOR MARINE LIFE,* she read, her heart quickening. *Marine biologists worldwide have expressed their concerns about the sudden disappearance of several species in our oceans…*the article began. Molly felt her spirits sink.

"Everything all right, there, Molls?" her mum asked, seeing the look on her face.

Molly forced the corners of her mouth to turn up in a fake smile. "Sure," she replied as brightly as she could. It wasn't the truth, though. Everything was definitely *not* all right, not in the slightest. Down in the ocean, strange and

worrying things had happened recently. All
the whales, dolphins, seahorses, penguins,
octopuses and turtles had completely
vanished. And how did Molly know this?
Because she was the secret mermaid. At night,
she sometimes visited the ocean as a mermaid,
thanks to the magic powers of a special piece
of shell Gran had given her.

Molly had been helping her friends, the
Animal-Keeper mermaids, find their missing
animals and so far, she'd helped to rescue the
seahorses, dolphins and penguins. Each time,
the creatures had been shrunk to tiny sizes
and then imprisoned in places which were
difficult to find. Molly and the other
mermaids had managed to set them free, and
they'd become their usual sizes once more.
But the whales, turtles and octopuses still
hadn't been found.

Not yet, anyway, Molly thought, with a determined feeling rising inside her. *But I'll try my hardest to make sure we* do *find them – and soon...*

As Molly got ready for bed, she hoped with all her heart that she'd be magically taken to the Undersea Kingdom for another adventure that night. The newspaper article had worried her, and she wanted to help find the whales, turtles and octopuses as quickly as possible. It hadn't been easy to find the hidden creatures so far, though. Each time she'd had an adventure with the Animal-Keeper mermaids, they had found scary monsters guarding the imprisoned sea creatures. She'd managed to defeat them so far with the help of a silver animal charm a walrus had given her back in the summer, but it didn't make her feel any more confident about facing another of the dangerous monsters...

Once she'd said goodnight to her parents and gran, she arranged her special necklace on her bedside table as usual. The silver animal charm hung next to the piece of magic conch shell on the chain and to look at them, you'd never know that they had such amazing powers. But the smooth piece of creamy-white shell had performed all sorts of incredible feats when Molly had needed it to, and she'd discovered that the animal charm had the power to grant her different animal abilities if she wished for them too.

She smiled sleepily as she remembered how wonderful it had been to swim as fast as a dolphin, and how weird it had felt when she'd been able to camouflage herself like a seahorse. And thank goodness the charm had given her the power to keep warm like a penguin, when she'd been inside that iceberg!

Just as she was thinking this, a faint pink light suddenly began to pulse from the piece of conch shell, making the silver charm glitter alongside it. Molly stiffened with excitement at the sight. The sparkling light that was now streaming from her shell could only mean one thing: another adventure was about to begin!

Chapter Two

Molly closed her eyes and immediately felt as if she were falling down a great hole. She knew that this was the mermaid magic at work, but it was still the strangest sensation – exhilarating and scary all at the same time. After a few moments, she could hear a rushing sound around her and knew, with a thrill of anticipation, that she was back in the ocean, and that she was a mermaid again,

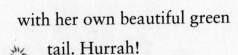

with her own beautiful green tail. Hurrah!

She opened her eyes and blinked, staring around the watery world. Often she found herself in an unfamiliar place at the start of her mermaid adventures – somewhere far out in the ocean, sometimes in tropical seas, sometimes in freezing waters. This time…

She smiled as she recognized the high, jewel-adorned ceiling above her head, and the glittering golden thrones across the grand underwater hall. This time, she knew exactly where she was – in the Merqueen's palace, right at the heart of the Undersea Kingdom! But why had she been brought here?

"My dear, it's good to have you back," came a voice, and Molly turned to see Queen Luna, the gracious mermaid queen, swimming towards her. The Merqueen was quite the most beautiful creature Molly had ever met, with her long chestnut-coloured hair twisted up elegantly on her head. Her eyes were wise, kind and understanding, and her voice was low and musical. Today, though, to Molly's dismay, the queen appeared grave and unhappy, her lovely face etched with lines of worry.

Molly opened her mouth to speak, then closed it again. She'd been about to ask if the queen was all right, but she wasn't sure that it was polite to ask a queen such a personal question. "Hello," she said instead, bobbing a neat curtsy.

The queen swam over and took her hands. "Thank you so much for your help with our sea creatures," she said, squeezing Molly's fingers gently. "We are all extremely grateful for your courage and quick-thinking in helping rescue so many of our animal friends. But there have been developments since you were last here. Come," she said, beckoning towards an open door. "The Animal-Keeper mermaids are waiting for us in the courtyard."

Molly followed the Merqueen out through the arching doorway into the pretty courtyard garden at the centre of the palace, where

exotic-looking emerald-green and rust-red
sea-plants rippled in the gentle current. In one
corner of the garden was a huge pink scallop
shell, with a cluster of large rocks around it
which were covered in soft velvety sea moss.
Sitting on the rocks were six other mermaids, all
gazing expectantly at Molly
and the Merqueen.

The mermaids were called Eloise, Shanti, Iona, Aisha, Phoebe and Leila, and they each looked after one of the groups of creatures that had recently vanished from the seas.

"Hi, guys," Molly said, smiling as she swam over to them.

"Hi, Molly," Phoebe and Aisha chorused, and the others smiled briefly, although they, too, seemed anxious.

Molly felt her insides turn over. Everybody seemed so solemn – had some other creatures gone missing now as well? What was going on?

"Do be seated," the Merqueen commanded, settling herself into the pink scallop shell. "We've had some bad news, I'm afraid. I know that when you and Phoebe were rescuing the penguins, you heard a rumour that the Dark Queen was back."

Molly nodded. The Dark Queen Carlotta was a bad mermaid, who'd caused all sorts of trouble within the Undersea Kingdom before. She had been banished back in the summer, and had her magical powers stripped from her. But when Molly and Phoebe had been on the trail of the missing penguins, they'd met a shoal of sardines, who'd described a dark-haired, hook-nosed mermaid they'd seen – and Molly had known instantly, with a lurch in her stomach, that they had been describing Carlotta.

"Well, unfortunately, that rumour is true," the Merqueen said with a sigh. "I've just witnessed the evidence for myself on the Seeing Stone here." She gestured to the large, white boulder on which images from around the ocean magically appeared at her command. "And she's not alone. I've seen images of strange, monster-like creatures alongside her – made from sand, mud, rock…"

"Ice, too," Phoebe put in, with a sideways look at Molly.

A shiver went down Molly's spine as she remembered the terrifying ice monster that had attacked her in a giant iceberg last time she'd been a mermaid.

"I am almost certain that it's the Dark Queen who has enchanted our creatures, shrunk them to tiny sizes and trapped them," the Merqueen went on. "My guess is that by doing so, she's sapping them of their life force, and using this energy to rebuild her strength and form her army of monsters."

"That's not all," Aisha put in. "Somehow she seems to have taken the animals' special powers away, too. My dolphins certainly aren't as fast as they once were, and I know that the penguins aren't so good at keeping themselves warm since they were rescued either."

"And the seahorses can no longer camouflage themselves by changing colour, as they used to," Eloise added dolefully.

"All this makes me wonder two things," the Merqueen went on. "Has the Dark Queen somehow managed to steal these special powers to use herself? And if so, how can we get them back?" She bit her lip. "Or are we too late?"

An uneasy silence fell over the mermaids. Nobody looked at all happy, and Molly felt anxious too. Whenever she'd used the animal charm so far, it had granted her those exact three powers – the ability to swim fast like a dolphin, keep herself warm in freezing temperatures like a penguin, and camouflage herself like a seahorse. She couldn't help worrying that *she* had sapped the animals' powers, by using the charm, even though the

26

mermaids had reassured her that this wasn't the case.

"Why is the Dark Queen doing all this, anyway?" Molly asked. "I don't understand."

"Nor do we," the Merqueen replied. "And that concerns me. She's clearly planning something big, for which she needs the special animal powers as well as this army of monsters...but exactly what she has in mind, we can only guess at."

A trickle of cold fear slid down Molly's back at her words. This sounded scarier and scarier.

"All we can do is to keep on looking for the missing creatures," the Merqueen went on. "And keep an eye out for any clues as to what Carlotta is plotting, as well." She knotted her fingers in her lap. "I'm afraid we need to expect the worst. She'll be seeking revenge, after we banished her, I am certain."

A sleek brown sea lion burst into the courtyard just then, his round eyes shining with excitement. "Your Majesty, there's urgent news just in," he honked breathlessly. "We've had reports of some strange eggs that have been found on the beach of a tropical island. They look like turtle eggs, but they're *sparkling*, apparently…"

"Ooh," Shanti said, leaning forwards, her blue eyes shining. She was the mermaid who

28

looked after the turtles, and had long red hair in two plaits, and pale skin, with freckles spattered across her cheeks. A silver pendant in the shape of a turtle hung around her neck. "Sparkling turtle eggs…that does sound interesting. I think I should take a look, to see if they're connected with my missing turtles in any way."

"I could come with you," Molly offered at once, and Shanti smiled at her.

"Thanks," she said. "I was hoping you'd say that."

Queen Luna still looked solemn, her lips pressed together in a thin line. "It definitely sounds worth investigating," she agreed, "but if these mysterious eggs *do* have anything to do with the missing turtles, then you can be sure that the Dark Queen will have ordered her monsters to guard them.

Molly knows how dangerous they are – you must both take great care."

Shanti nodded, leaping from her position on the rock and swimming over to Molly. "We'll be careful," she promised, holding a hand out to Molly. "Are you ready? Then let's go."

Chapter Three

Molly swam with Shanti out of the palace and through the golden gates that marked the boundary of the Undersea Kingdom. Then they were into the open ocean, swimming breathtakingly fast through the clear blue waters. Molly loved swimming as a mermaid. Her tail was so powerful and muscular that the merest of flicks sent her whizzing at great speed over the rocks and sand of the seabed below.

After they'd been swimming for some time, the temperature of the water rose and Molly knew they must be heading into tropical seas. Now there was a vast stretch of coral reef below them, with fish of all colours and sizes darting through the maze of green, purple, yellow and red coral tunnels. Molly saw jellyfish, clown fish and blue-spotted puffer fish, as well as spiny sea urchins and flower-like anemones in many shades.

"This reef is usually full of turtles," Shanti said as they swam above it. "It breaks my heart, seeing it empty of them like this."

"It's not right," Molly agreed, thinking of the friendly turtles she'd met when she'd helped another mermaid, Coral, save some endangered reefs in the summer. She and Coral had found a tiny, lost turtle – the cutest thing ever! – and had reunited him with his mum. "The sooner we find all those turtles and get them back where they belong, the better."

Shanti nodded. "Absolutely," she said.

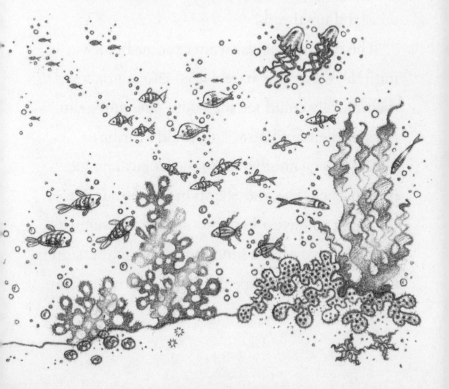

Then she stopped swimming and stared around, as if getting her bearings. "This way, I think," she said, pointing left. "We must be nearly there now."

Molly followed Shanti as she veered to the left. The water was becoming lighter and lighter and the seabed shelved sharply upwards. "Not too fast," Shanti warned Molly, slowing once again. "We're coming into shallower waters now. There's an island up ahead."

The two mermaids swam cautiously forwards until the water was barely deep enough to cover them. Molly could see the white sand and palm trees of the island now, and could hear birds calling to one another from the tropical jungle further back. She and Shanti broke the surface of the water to have a better look. The hot sun was beating down on the sand, but the beach was quite empty, without a single person or animal in sight.

It was the sort of beach Molly had only
seen in holiday brochures, with
its fine pale sand, crystal-clear
blue waters lapping at the edge,
and the fringe of palm trees
laden with coconuts, their
huge leaves creating spiky
shadows on the ground.

But she wasn't here to think about holidays, of course. There was work to be done. They scoured the edge of the beach, searching for signs of eggs. Molly opened her mouth to say, "There!" a couple of times before realizing that what she'd just seen were gleaming white shells that had been washed up by the tide.

"What do turtle eggs look like?" she asked Shanti. "How big are they?"

"They look—" Shanti began, and then her
finger shot out to point further along the beach.
"They look like *that*," she finished with an
excited laugh, and Molly saw them – a clutch of
round white eggs, barely visible, as they were
half-buried in the sand. Molly's heart raced as
she noticed the faint shimmering light around the
eggs, just as the sea lion had said. A shimmering
light which might very well suggest magic!

"Come on, let's have a proper look," Shanti said, ducking under the water and surging nearer the shoreline like a silver streak.

Molly didn't wait to be told twice. She followed Shanti until they were as near as they could get to the eggs, then peeped out of the water to see them more closely. She counted six of them, set a few metres up the beach, smooth and white, roughly the size of ping-pong balls.

"Ooh, I've got a good feeling about this," Shanti said. "They're definitely turtle eggs, but the way they're sparkling like that...they look magical to me. As if they'd been enchanted, even..."

"I agree," Molly said excitedly. "So maybe the sea turtles have been shrunk down to teeny-weeny sizes, and are trapped inside them!"

"We've *got* to get hold of them, to see!" Shanti cried, waving her hands expressively as she spoke and splashing the water.

The sound seemed loud against the quiet of the beach, and Molly pulled Shanti back under the water. "Remember what the Merqueen told us," she whispered. "There may be more of Carlotta's monsters guarding the eggs – we've got to be quiet. And quick!"

Shanti clapped a hand over her mouth, looking nervous. "Oops,"

she said in a low voice. "So how are we going to get the eggs?" she hissed. "They're too far up the beach for us – we won't be able to breathe long enough out of the water to slither across the sand and grab them."

"Could we ask one of the gulls?" Molly suggested, hearing one screeching overhead. "Maybe it could pick up the eggs in its beak and drop them into the water for us."

Shanti shook her head. "I don't trust them," she whispered. "Horrible things."

"Some gulls helped me and Aisha set the dolphins free," Molly said. "They were grumpy at first, but when they saw my animal charm, they did the job straight away."

Shanti didn't look convinced. "Even so... seagulls eat hundreds of tiny turtle hatchlings – I don't want them going anywhere near *those* eggs. Imagine – if all the turtles *are* trapped in there, and one stupid greedy gull gobbled them down! They'd be lost for ever, then – every last one." She shook her head again. "Once the turtles are full size and have their strong, hard shells, only a few creatures in the ocean – some sharks and whales – dare attack them. But when they're tiny, they're so vulnerable, poor things. We're going to have to be very careful, Molly. We've got to get this right."

Molly thought hard. "Well, if we can't get *over* the sand, maybe we should go *under* it," she reasoned. "If we could get something to tunnel through the sand, perhaps, and burrow up beneath the eggs so that they can plop into the hole and roll down into the water..."

"Yes!" Shanti exclaimed, then remembered to lower her voice. "We can ask the crabs to help us," she began more quietly, but then frowned. "No, we can't," she corrected herself.

"*They* eat turtle eggs as well." Then she grinned suddenly as a thought struck her. "Ahh! Got it! The sand eels!"

"Sand eels?" Molly echoed.

"Yes," Shanti said. "They're excellent little burrowers. If we have enough of them together at once, they should be able to help us get the eggs. Cool!"

"Good thinking." Molly smiled. Shanti's enthusiasm was infectious. "And where do we find these sand eels?"

Shanti pointed to the seabed. "In the sand!" she replied. "Let me see if I can call a few up."

She swam a little deeper and began singing in a strange language Molly couldn't understand. Her voice was rich and melodious, and the sound of the lilting song made goosebumps prickle along Molly's arms.

Then Molly jumped as she saw a silvery head

emerge from the sand below. With a wriggle,
the creature pulled itself right out of the seabed,
and Molly could see that it was a small,
silver-grey eel, about the length of her
dad's hand. Out came another. And
another – and another – and soon
the water around them was a
mass of writhing, squirming
sand eels, all seeming to
dance to the melody
of Shanti's song.

Shanti stopped singing, but before she could speak to them, the sand eels swarmed towards Molly and peered at the animal charm on her necklace.

The walrus who had given Molly the charm had declared her a friend of sea creatures everywhere, and assured her that if she was ever in trouble while in the ocean, the sea creatures would always do their best to assist her. And that had been the case every time so far. Once animals recognized the silver charm, they couldn't do enough for her.

"Oooh!" the sand eels squealed in thin, reedy voices, jostling each other with excitement as they saw it now. They bowed their snakelike heads before her. "Gracious mistress! What is your bidding? We are at your command!"

"Thank you," Molly said, mesmerized by the sea of rippling silver bodies around her.

"Thank you. Um…I've heard you're the best burrowers in the ocean—"

"We are, gracious mistress!" the sand eels chorused, still bobbing their heads up and down.

"So I was wondering if you could all burrow into the sand over here for us," Molly went on, pointing, "in order to tunnel under the eggs on the beach up here." She rose to the surface, followed by the mass of sand eels, and pointed at where the eggs lay on the sand.

"We see, gracious mistress," the sand eels chorused, diving below the surface again, still somehow managing to nod as they did so.

"Do you think you can do it?" Shanti asked eagerly.

"We'll try, mermaid mistresses!" they cried as one, darting down to the seabed and beginning to burrow.

The sand eels were amazing, Molly thought, watching their silver bodies squirming into the sand. Before long they'd all vanished from sight. "Brilliant," she said happily. This was all working out perfectly!

"Now I guess we just have to wait," Shanti said, after a few moments. "Wait and hope, cross our fingers and— Oh!" She broke off suddenly as several silvery heads popped back out of the sand. "Everything all right?" she asked in concern.

The sand eels seemed droopy with disappointment. "We tried, mermaid mistresses," they chorused, "but…"

A single sand eel pushed himself forward. "It was too far," he said, his head down. "The sand became dry. We couldn't breathe."

"We're sorry, mermaid mistresses," the other sand eels said miserably.

"We're really sorry," echoed the sand eel who'd spoken alone. "We've let you down. The mermaid mistress with the animal charm asked us for help – and we failed her!"

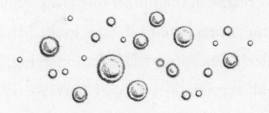

Chapter Four

"You didn't!" Molly cried at once, feeling sorry for them. They looked so defeated. "You did your best – you haven't let anybody down. It was silly of us not to think about something so basic as breathing when we wouldn't even be able to breathe in the tunnel ourselves." She patted the nearest sand eel, who looked particularly mournful. "Thanks for trying. You're all very kind – and very brave."

"Absolutely," Shanti added. She was trying to sound hearty, but her eyes were clouded with disappointment. "No worries, guys. We'll think of something else."

The sand eels slipped back into the sand, and silence fell. Shanti let herself drop to the seabed, looking glum. "Any ideas?" she asked, fiddling with a nearby razor shell.

"Well, we know now that burrowing to get the eggs from under the sand isn't going to work," Molly reasoned. "Let's go back to thinking of ways to get them *over* the sand. We just need something to roll them down to the sea for us."

"Mmm," Shanti agreed, twirling the razor shell around her fingers as she thought.

"If we could somehow rig up some kind of chute…" Molly began, and then her eyes fell on the razor shell in Shanti's hand. Shanti had one half of the shell, and it was long and slightly curved, rather like a tiny gutter. Molly's mind worked furiously. "You know…when Eloise and I rescued the seahorses, they were trapped inside a bubble," she said, thinking aloud. "We used some mermaid magic together to make a crab so big it could burst the bubble with its pincers."

Shanti looked baffled. "We can't ask a gigantic crab to move the eggs," she reminded Molly. "It'll eat them!"

Molly shook her head. "I don't mean that," she said. "How about we magic that razor shell bigger? So big it could act like a sort of chute – a slide! We could push it out onto the beach, tuck one end under the eggs, then tilt the other end down, so that the eggs—"

"Would roll down the shell to us!" Shanti finished, leaping up delightedly. "Molly, you're a genius!"

"Shall we try it, then?" Molly asked.

"Absolutely!" Shanti replied.

She grabbed the razor shell in one hand, and her silver pendant with the other, then began muttering a magical command.

A stream of jade-green sparkles shot out of Shanti's pendant and swirled all around the razor shell. It immediately grew to be a metre long, and Shanti almost dropped it in shock. "Whoa!" she cried, her eyes shining. Then she grinned at Molly. "Let's make it even bigger," she decided, repeating the magic words under her breath.

More of the green sparkles poured from the centre of her silver pendant, covering the razor shell in twinkling lights. Once again, it grew in size, so big and so quickly, Molly had to dodge out of the way. Now it was about six metres long and at least a metre wide, and looked like the coolest water slide – or rather, *egg* slide – that Molly had ever seen.

"Perfect," she said, smiling.

"Looks good to me," Shanti agreed, holding one side of it. "Let's push it up the beach. Ready? One...two...three...heave!"

They both shoved the massive shell-slide over the sand. As it neared the eggs, they pushed it more slowly and cautiously, their eyes above the surface of the water so that they could see. "We do *not* want to squish those eggs," Shanti said firmly. "Not after all this!"

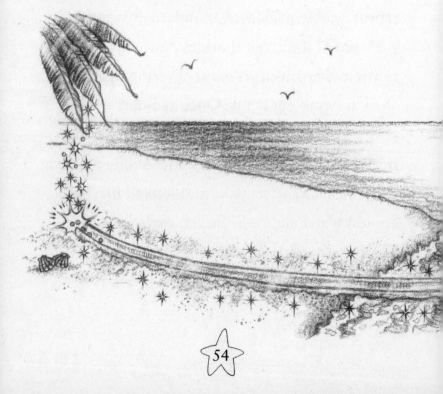

"A bit more," Molly said, peering up the beach and trying to judge the exact distance. "Nearly there, just a tiny bit more…"

They had to get the shell's far edge to scoop up the eggs, but they knew they had to do it very, very carefully. The shell was so big and cumbersome now that delicate little movements were very tricky to achieve. "One last teeny-weeny baby push…" Molly said, holding her breath as they manoeuvred the shell another few centimetres.

Up it went…just a tiny bit more…and…

"Yes!" Shanti yelled in triumph as they managed to scoop the eggs with the lip of the shell. "We got it – they're all on the chute!"

Molly grinned at her. "Now we just need to tip our end of the chute *down*…" she said, pushing it lower in the water, "and…"

"Here they come!" Shanti whooped, ducking underwater again. "Oh my goodness!" she cheered as, slowly but surely, the turtle eggs started to roll towards them down their razor-shell chute. "It's actually working!"

Molly could hardly breathe with excitement as the little white eggs came nearer and

nearer, trundling merrily along the slippery slide. Then with a series of delicate plops, they splashed into the water – and Shanti's waiting hands.

"Result!" cheered Shanti happily. "Oh, Molly, you are a total genius. Well done, you!"

Molly beamed, thrilled that the plan had worked. "Now to find out what is *inside* these eggs," she said hopefully, and lifted one of them from Shanti's hands. It felt soft and rubbery in her grasp and she held her breath as she raised it to her ear and listened. She could just make out faint voices from inside:

"What's happened?"

"Thank goodness that rolling has stopped!"

"It doesn't feel so hot any more, does it?"

"It's them!" Molly said to Shanti in delight, holding the egg to her friend's ear. "It's the turtles!"

Tears rushed to Shanti's eyes as she too heard the creatures' tiny voices. But then Molly

heard something else. A faint creaking sound –
coming from the direction of the reef. What
was it?

She turned and stared. The creaking was
getting louder. Now it sounded like bones
rattling. Molly gulped as she saw something
move. Rising up from the reef were a dozen
looming white creatures. Monsters!

"Shanti – look!" Molly hissed. "Monsters –
it looks as if they're made from the coral!"

She stared, her heart beating hard. The
creatures were striding slowly towards the
mermaids in a long line. They were roughly
man-shaped, with two long legs, two arms and a
head each, but their bodies seemed to be formed
of twisty white branches of coral, so that they
resembled creepy walking skeletons. Sinister
yellow eyes glowed in their faces as they strode
forward, the coral creaking and rattling with
each movement.

"Oh my goodness!" Shanti gasped, her face turning even paler than usual. She held the eggs close to her body. "Well, they're not getting their hands on *these* – no way!"

Molly nodded, her throat tight with fear. Then she saw something that scared her even more. "Look," she hissed. "They're carrying weapons!"

The monsters were each brandishing coral axes and spears, and were now shaking them threateningly at the mermaids as they stomped ever nearer in a long, menacing line.

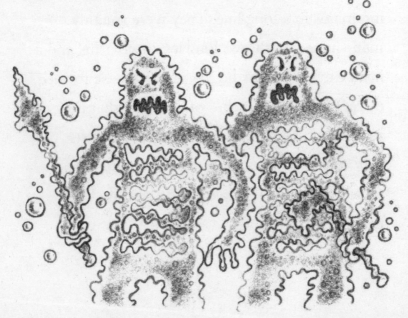

"Come on," Shanti said urgently, passing Molly some of the eggs. "Let's get out of here – fast!"

She swerved to the left of the line of reef-monsters, swimming diagonally away from the island. Molly followed, her heart thumping, but as she and Shanti swam over the reef, more of the coral-monsters appeared, rising up like ghosts, their coral bones making a horrible clattering noise as they moved.

Molly let out a scream, trying to swim even faster as she saw the coral-monsters raising the spears and axes in their hands, and throwing them at the mermaids. Molly and Shanti dodged the missiles as best they could, zigzagging over the reef, but whichever way they turned, more and more of the monsters appeared, their yellow eyes shining through the water.

"There are loads of them!" Shanti cried in terror. "And this reef goes on for ever – we're never going to get out!"

Molly thought frantically, then remembered her magical animal charm that was swinging from her necklace. In the past, its magic had worked almost accidentally – she'd been wishing for something, and she'd been granted a particular animal ability that answered her wish. So what could she ask for this time?

It was hard to think straight; lumps of coral were flying around her as the monsters threw their missiles more forcefully than ever, and it was all Molly could do to keep going, let alone form a plan.

"Ow!" she cried, as a coral spear grazed her tail, and she felt a stinging pain. In the next moment, a scream went up from Shanti as a stone smacked the back of her head – and then she went limp in the water.

Molly's heart pounded with fright as she swam over to her friend. "Shanti! Are you all right?" she cried, clutching at her arm.

But Shanti didn't respond. Her eyes were closed and her body wasn't moving.

The eggs slipped from her hand and panic rushed through Molly. "Shanti! Can you hear me?" she yelled, feeling sick with fear. She turned to see that the monsters were closing in, too many of them to count, their eyes glinting with menace, their coral bones clattering horribly. What could she do? What could she *do?*

Chapter Five

We need some kind of shield, Molly thought desperately, as another missile struck her hard between the shoulder blades. She had to keep them both from being hit while she got Shanti and the eggs to safety...

Then something Shanti had said earlier came back to her, about how the turtles protected themselves. Of course! She grabbed the silver charm. "I wish I had some armour, like a turtle's shell!" she shouted, the words leaving her mouth in wobbling silver bubbles.

The charm felt burning hot between her fingers, and Molly saw a hologram of a turtle appear on its smooth surface. Then she felt a peculiar sensation all the way down her back and tail, as if she were completely numb there. She glanced over her shoulder and saw what looked like enchanted armour covering her body. Yes – perfect!

Turning slightly, she angled her body so that the armour was towards the monsters, and immediately heard the rattle of their weapons and missiles bouncing against it. She couldn't feel a thing now though – the enchanted armour was keeping her completely safe.

She grabbed Shanti and pulled her close, so that Shanti was protected as well. Missile after missile slammed against the force field created by the magical armour but fell back without hurting either of them.

Molly gathered up all the eggs and tucked them between her body and Shanti's, hoping she'd be able to keep them there without losing or squashing them. "Now I need to get us out of here," she muttered to herself, one arm around Shanti's limp body. "I don't know how long this magic will last."

It was hard work swimming with Shanti and the eggs, and Molly's sore tail was really throbbing by the time she reached the end of the coral reef. Thankfully, although there were lots of them, the monsters were slow-moving, and Molly finally managed to get clear of the reef and a safe distance away from them and their missiles.

She sank to the ground behind a large black boulder, panting with exhaustion as she caught her breath. She'd managed to get away from the monsters, at least, but she still had the problem of Shanti's injury to deal with – and the turtle eggs to keep safe. Luckily, at that moment, Shanti stirred...and then opened her eyes.

"Ow," she said, blinking and rubbing the back of her head. Then she stared around. "Where are we? What happened?"

Molly was so thankful to see Shanti moving and speaking again that she hugged her, not able to speak at first. "Thank goodness you're all right," she said, almost crying with relief as she went on to explain her terrifying escape from the coral-monsters.

"Oh, Molly," Shanti said, her face as white as chalk. "You saved my life. You're so brave – thank you a million times!"

Molly managed a smile. "It could have been worse," she said, and showed Shanti where the eggs were safely piled on the sand. "We've still got these little guys."

"Oh, well done," Shanti sighed. "Now we've got to set the turtles free as quickly as we can – before those coral-monsters find us!"

Molly picked up one of the eggs and tapped it gently against the rock, hoping to crack it like a hen's egg. The shell was soft and leathery though, rather than hard and brittle, and it didn't break.

She was just looking around for something to help her open the eggs, when she remembered how the chick had tapped its way out of its own egg at the farm that morning, using its beak to crack the shell. "How do baby turtles hatch usually?" she asked Shanti.

"They have a little egg tooth on their noses," Shanti replied. "They tap at the egg from the inside with the egg tooth, and that breaks it open." She shrugged. "But the turtles in these eggs won't have their egg teeth any more, they only last a few weeks."

"Is there anything else they could tap at the shell with?" Molly wondered. "There must be thousands of tiny turtles in each egg and I'm just thinking, if they all tapped at the eggs together…"

Shanti looked more cheerful. "They have claws on their front flippers – they're strong and powerful. That might work!" She held each egg up to her mouth in turn and told the turtles the plan. "So on my count, you've all got to tap against the inside," she said. "Really go for it, as hard as you can. Ready, guys? One, two, three…TAP! One, two, three…TAP!"

The eggs shook violently each time she said "Tap!" as every turtle bashed against the shell. Then, on the third count, a small crack appeared along the length of one egg. "Keep going! One, two, three…TAP!" called Shanti, her voice bubbling with excitement.

Cracks were appearing on the other eggs now.

"One, two, three…TAP!" Shanti called encouragingly. "Come on, it's working!"

To Molly's delight, a small hole had appeared in one egg now and she couldn't resist gently picking at it to make it bigger.

Very carefully, she pulled the sides of the hole apart, until the egg split right open…and out poured a stream of tiny turtles!

As they rejoined the ocean, the turtles grew

bigger and bigger and bigger. More eggs broke,
and Molly and Shanti were soon surrounded
by countless sea turtles, all swimming freely
and happily.

Molly was delighted to recognize the mother and son turtles she'd met in the summer – goodness, the baby turtle had grown! – and swam over to them. "Hello! How are you? Are you all right?" she cried.

The mother turtle was gazing around, looking rather confused, but her eyes twinkled when she saw Molly. "Hello, my dear," she said, putting a flipper around Molly's back. "It's lovely to see you again." But when Molly hugged the mother turtle she was dismayed to feel the mother's shell.

It wasn't as hard as it usually was – in fact, it felt soft and spongy. "Oh dear, this isn't right," she said anxiously, and one look at Shanti's face told Molly that her friend had made the same discovery.

"Listen, guys," Shanti was calling. "You're going to have to be very careful – your shells are soft and you'll be vulnerable to predators without your usual protection. Hopefully in time your shells will toughen up again but until then…"

A very old-looking turtle with the wrinkliest face Molly had ever seen raised a flipper and interrupted. "I don't think so," he said, in a creaky voice. "That's why she did it, you see. The Dark Queen. That's why she trapped us."

Molly stared. None of the creatures she'd set free before had ever been able to remember any details about what had happened to them. "What do you mean?" she asked.

Shanti had heard too. "This is Corinthius," she explained quickly. "Our oldest and wisest turtle with an amazing memory. If anyone can solve the mystery it's him." She gave his shell a loving stroke. "Hello there," she said. "Do you remember what happened?"

The old turtle blinked. "The Dark Queen summoned us all to a cave with her bad magic," he explained, his words coming out slowly. "We couldn't fight it – the enchantment was too strong." He blinked again.

"Then she used her magic to leach us of our armour powers," he went on, still in that creaky voice.

"The armour power rose up from us like a vapour – and she collected that vapour in a small bottle, and tied it around her waist. As long as she has the armour power, we will be without it."

Shanti took his flipper in her hand. "Do you remember anything else, Corinthius?" she asked.

The wise old turtle shook his head. "Everything is a blur after that," he replied.

Molly and Shanti looked at one another.

"We'll do our best to get your armour power back," Molly promised.

Shanti nodded. "But in the meantime, you must take great care," she said. "Stay away from the sharks, stick together in groups, look after one another."

Molly was about to speak when she saw the bright light of dawn shining down through the water, and she knew that her magical adventure was almost at an end. She hugged Shanti quickly. "Take care," she called to the turtles. "I'll be back to help as soon as I can!"

But before she could say another word, she felt as if her whole body was being pulled very hard and very fast, out of the ocean and away.

Molly woke up the next morning feeling anxious. She hated to think of the turtles being weak and defenceless without their tough shells to protect them, and couldn't get her mind off what the wise turtle had said, about the Dark Queen stripping the turtles of their power and storing it in a bottle.

Presumably this was what she'd done to the other creatures too – the dolphins, seahorses and penguins – so that she had their special powers for herself, as well as extra strength to create her army of monsters! But what was she planning to do with those powers? Was she plotting to steal the pieces of the magic conch shell again – or something even worse?

Molly sat up, and as she did so, saw a faint red scratch down her left leg. She stared at it,

puzzled. Where had that come from? Then
she remembered how one of the reef monsters'
coral spears had scraped her mermaid tail
on the left side. So injuries she got in the

Undersea Kingdom were carried over into the human world – well, it made sense, she supposed. But it also meant that if something really bad happened to her during a mermaid adventure, then…

She got out of bed, not wanting to think about that. There was no point worrying about what might happen, was there? The fact was, the whales and octopuses were still missing somewhere, and Molly *had* to help the Animal-Keeper mermaids find them and set them free. She also had to find out more about the bottle the wise turtle had seen, containing the animals' powers. If Molly and her mermaid friends could somehow take it from the Dark Queen, then they might be able to restore the animals to full strength – but doing so would surely mean getting up close to the Dark Queen herself. That wasn't exactly a prospect Molly relished!

She gazed out of the window at the cold, wintry sea below, hoping the turtles were keeping safe. *I'll make sure they get their armour power back*, she vowed to herself. *Even if it does mean taking on the Dark Queen – I'm ready!*

The End

Read on for a sneak preview of Molly's next magical underwater adventure...

Whale Rescue

"Do you want a mince pie, Molly? Gran and I
made them while you were at school, and
they're still warm."

Molly looked up at the sound of her mum's
voice. It was a December afternoon and she was
lying on the living room floor writing Christmas
cards to her friends. "Yes, please," she said,
unable to resist the tantalizing smell of spicy
fruit and pastry that was wafting through from
the kitchen.

She sat up as her mum passed her a bowl filled with two mince pies and cream, and dug a spoon in hungrily. "Mmm," she said at the first mouthful. Now she felt *really* Christmassy! She and her parents had decorated the house last night with sprays of holly, and strings of red and gold sparkly tinsel, and it looked so pretty. At school, they had been practising the Christmas play every day, and had made all sorts of glitter-covered pictures and gifts to take home at the end of term. Molly always loved this time of year, but the parties and carol concerts and the fun things she'd been doing at school made it feel extra special.

Her eye fell on the pile of Christmas cards on the floor. That made her feel happy too – that she had so many friends to give cards to now. Molly's family had moved to Horseshoe Bay back in the summer and, at first, she'd missed her friends from her old school and had been rather lonely. Now she was much more settled in her new school, and was enjoying getting to know the girls in her class. And of course, ever since she'd become the Secret Mermaid she had her mermaid friends too...and the times she'd spent with them had been the most wonderful and exciting experiences of her life!

Gran made her way slowly into the living room just then, leaning on her stick, and put the television on before sinking into the sofa. "You've been busy," she commented, indicating the pile of cards on the floor. "I hope there's one for me there, too."

Molly smiled at her gran. "You get a special one," she told her, thinking about the snowflake cards she'd painted at school, one for each member of her family – even Toby, her baby brother. Gran deserved an especially nice present, Molly thought to herself. After all, it had been Gran who'd given Molly her best gift ever – the magic shell necklace that took her into the mermaid world of the Undersea Kingdom, where Molly had had so many amazing adventures.

Gran was watching a news programme on the television, and Molly found herself half-listening as she finished her mince pies (delicious!) and went back to writing cards.

Dear Tess, Happy Christmas, Love—

But then her attention was caught by something the news reporter said, and Molly's pen almost skidded off the paper as she looked up at the screen.

"At this time of year, here on the Pacific Coast of Mexico, you can usually see hundreds of grey whales arriving from their feeding grounds of Alaska, as part of their annual migration," the reporter was saying. He was standing on a deserted beach, gesturing at the empty blue sea behind him. "The whales migrate from the cooler waters where they feed in the summer months, to warmer waters, such as this part of the ocean, in winter months, to give birth to their young. But this year, their migration pattern seems to have changed," he went on, sounding concerned. "There's no sign of any whales here yet – and we've had similar reports from other migration hot spots around the world." He frowned into the camera, holding his hands wide. "The question is, where are all the whales – and what does this mean for their future?"

An icy chill went down Molly's back as she watched some old footage of the whales joyfully leaping high out of the water – or breaching, as she had learned it was called. *She* knew what had happened to the whales, of course. They had been captured by Carlotta, a bad mermaid, who called herself the Dark Queen.

To find out what happens next, read

The Secret Mermaid

Whale Rescue

To find out more
about Molly and all her
mermaid friends, and have
some magical ocean fun,
check out
www.thesecretmermaid.co.uk

Collect all of Molly's magical mermaid adventures

Enchanted Shell ◎ 9780746096154

Molly is transported to the Undersea Kingdom for the first time, where she discovers she is the secret mermaid!

Seaside Adventure ◎ 9780746096161

To help Ella recover her piece of the magical conch, Molly must find a way to trap an angry killer whale.

Underwater Magic ◎ 9780746096178

Can Molly find some pirate treasure to win back Delphi's shell from a grumpy sea urchin?

Reef Rescue ◎ 9780746096192

Molly must help Coral find her shell to restore the ocean reefs, but a swarm of jellyfish stands in their way…

Deep Trouble ◎ 9780746096185

Pearl's conch piece is trapped in an undersea volcano and guarded by sea snakes. How can she and Molly release it?

Return of the Dark Queen ◎ 9780746096208

Molly must save Shivana from an Arctic prison before the Shell-Keeper mermaids can finally face the Dark Queen and complete the magical conch.